Discovering Science Secrets

by Sandra Markle
Pictures by June Otani

SCHOLASTIC INC.

New York Toronto London Auckland Sydney

For Mary Dalheim,
whose creativity is always
an inspiration

ISBN 0-590-43515-9

12 11 10 9 8 7 6 5 4 3 2 1   1 2 3 4 5 6/9

Printed in the U.S.A.

First Scholastic printing, January 1991

Contents

Can you make a candle flame go out as if by magic?

Can you change milk into glue?

Can you put fizz in a fruit-flavored drink?

Can you create a chemical reaction that will power a toy boat?

Yes, you can do all this and more! All you need are some materials you will find at home or can purchase cheaply at a grocery or hobby store. Then perform the activities to find out how science can help you do some exciting things.

There are some quick quizzes to challenge you, too. They'll open your eyes to some amazing facts about plants and animals.

Remember

- Do not do any activity involving a flame without an adult to help you.
- Clean up the work area after you finish your project.
- Have fun!

Find Out What Won't Mix

A great many things mix so completely that they seem to disappear when they are stirred into water. You've probably noticed that this happens to sugar and salt. When this happens, the substance is said to *dissolve*, and the mixture that results is called a *solution*. Mixing lemon juice and sugar with water makes a tasty solution — lemonade.

Most liquids dissolve in water, but not all do. And liquids that won't dissolve in water all have something in common. When you find out what that is, you'll be able to use this information to do something very special — print a colorful design on paper.

First, you need to test some liquids to discover which ones won't dissolve in water. To do this, pour two tablespoonsful of each of the liquids listed below into identical glasses or clear plastic cups full of water. Next, stir each glass while counting to five. Then wait one minute and look closely. Has the liquid you added mixed with the water or did it separate?

Test Liquids

Grape or
   orange juice
Red, blue, or green
   food coloring
Pancake syrup
Mineral oil

Melted margarine
Vegetable oil
Dark-colored
   soft drink
Coffee

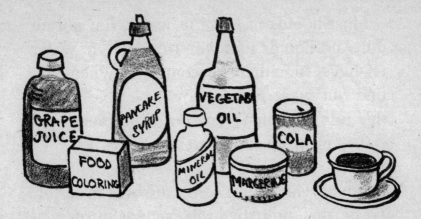

Now group together the cups containing the liquids that wouldn't dissolve in water. Rub a little bit of each of these liquids between your thumb and finger. All these liquids will feel oily.

Everything is made up of tiny building blocks called *molecules*. The molecules of liquids that dissolve in water easily separate and mix with the water to form a solution. But the molecules of oils and oil-base liquids, such as vegetable oil, stick together. So when these liquids are added to water, they form a separate layer. Because oily liquids are usually lighter than water, this layer floats on the surface.

Print with Water

In the experiment you just performed, you discovered that oil-base liquids separate and float on the surface when mixed with water. So, oil-base hobby paint will float on water, too. You can use this science fact to create swirling, colorful designs on paper.

You'll need an aluminum pie pan, water (use distilled water if your local water contains a lot of minerals or chemicals), two or three different colors of oil-base hobby paints, scissors, white typing paper, toothpicks, and newspapers.

Small bottles of oil-base hobby paints are inexpensive. You can find them at stores that sell hobby and craft supplies. Since these paints will also color your clothing, wear an old shirt as a coverup while you work.

Start by covering your work area with newspapers. Set the pie pan on the newspapers and fill it about two-thirds full of water. Next, cut several sheets of typing paper in half. Cut each of these pieces in half again to make your printing sheets.

When you're ready to print, drip several small droplets of each color of paint onto the water. They'll float.

Draw a toothpick through the paint, swirling the colors and creating a design. As soon as you see a pattern you like, take one of the pieces of paper, holding it by diagonally opposite corners, and place it on the water's surface.

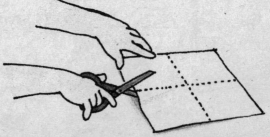

Count to three before lifting the paper off the water. Then turn your printed paper over and lay it — printed side up — on the newspaper to dry. Because the paper didn't soak up the water, it will dry remarkably flat.

You'll be able to print several pieces of paper before you need to add more paint to the water. Be creative. See how many different patterns you can design with your water printer.

People have been using the science fact that oil-base paints float on water to print paper this way for a very long time — since the 1600s. The result is called marbleized paper. It became the favorite method for decorating the endpapers of books and even the edges of the pages. How this effect was produced was kept a carefully guarded secret that was passed on only within families until the middle of the nineteenth century. And now you know it, too!

Master bookmakers used combs and special rakes to create specific marbleized patterns. Favorite patterns that were repeated over and over were given names such as *snail, peacock, feather,* and *agate.*

When your special printed paper is dry, you're ready to use it to decorate your book covers, to make greeting cards, or to trim stationery. You'll need glue for this, though. So let science help you make some.

Cook Up Moo Glue*

You don't ever have to run out of glue once you know the science for making glue from milk.

You'll need:

1½ cups 2% lowfat milk
¼ cup vinegar
½ teaspoon baking soda
Water
Saucepan
2 metal spoons

Pot holder
Cooling rack
1 empty quart jar
1 coffee filter
1 funnel

Pour the lowfat milk into the pan and add the vinegar. Stir over low heat, until tiny lumps form. The vinegar causes the

*You'll need to use the stove, so ask an adult to be your partner and work with you on this activity.

milk to *curdle* and the lumps are called *curds*.

Keep on stirring for several more minutes until no more curds appear to be developing. Use the pot holder to move the pan to the cooling rack. Let it sit for about 15 minutes.

Now you'll see that the curds have settled to the bottom, leaving a liquid called *whey* on top. Fit the coffee filter into the funnel and place the funnel in the quart jar. Pour the curds and the whey from the pan into the filter. The curds will remain in the filter and the whey will drain through, into the jar. Using a spoon or your fingers, press the

curds to make sure all the liquid comes out. Then dump the curds back into the pan.

Feel the curds. Do they remind you of a soft cheese? The process of making cheese also begins by curdling milk.

Next, add the one-half teaspoon of baking soda, mix well, and feel the soft curds again. They'll feel spongy this time.

Finally, stir in the water, one teaspoon at a time, until the mixture looks like glue. About two to three teaspoons should be enough.

Now try it out by gluing one of your printed papers to a sheet of white typing paper.

You can store leftover glue in a small jar with a tight lid for a few days. After that, it starts to smell bad.

Milk can be used to make glue because it contains a kind of protein called *casein*. Proteins, which can also be found in such foods as flour and eggs, form long chains of molecules. These chains are called *polymers*. Because polymers are naturally flexible, stretchy, and resist being pulled apart, they make good glue. The trick is to separate the protein molecules from the liquid part of the milk.

Usually, casein molecules repel each other and float separately in the milk liquid. However, when milk is mixed with vinegar and heated, the protein chains clump together, forming curds. Then, as you saw, you can easily drain off the liquid part of the milk and collect the curds of protein molecules. The baking soda stops the chemical reaction so no new curds form.

Moo glue is a strong glue. It's even waterproof. To prove this to yourself, use some moo glue to stick two pieces of notebook paper together. After the glue has completely dried, soak the papers in water for one minute. The two pieces of paper will remain stuck tight even when wet.

Purrfectly True — or Is It?

According to one superstition, cats have nine lives. That isn't true, but little or big, tame or wild, cats are all especially adapted for survival. For example, a tiger's stripes make it blend in perfectly with patches of light and shadow as it stalks its prey in tall jungle grass. The Canadian lynx, which does most of its hunting in snowy country, has extra big paws with fur pads to help it run across frozen ground.

Want to track down more amazing cat facts? Then don't miss this quiz.

1. House cats could roar if they felt like it. True or false?

2. One kind of cat has curly hair. True or false?

3. All cats can retract their claws, pulling them back into folds between their toes. True or false?

4. Cats always live and hunt alone. True or false?

5. Cats have whiskers just for looks. True or false?

1. *House cats could roar if they felt like it. True or false? False.* Domestic house cats can meow, hiss, scream, yowl, and much more to express their affection, anger, pleasure, and dislike. But they can't roar. They lack the elastic ligament supporting their tongue that all the big cats have. This ligament is what makes it possible for the big cats to produce such big sounds. A lion's thunderous voice has been recorded up to three miles away. So it's probably a good thing that house cats can't roar.

2. *One kind of cat has curly hair. True or false? True.* Rex cats are known for their naturally curly hair. Unlike most cats, which have long guard hairs and short downy hairs, this cat's fur is all short. The result is a wavy look. Even their whiskers and eyebrows are crinkled. This condition first developed as a mutation, which is a change that first showed up by chance. Then it was controlled by careful breeding.

At least the Rex has hair. Another breed, called the sphynx, is completely hairless.

3. *All cats can retract their claws, pulling them back into folds between their toes. True or false? False.* Cheetahs, unlike all the other members of the cat family, cannot retract their claws. This helps these big cats, however. Cheetahs, the fastest land animals, have been clocked at speeds of over 60 miles per hour. Short, blunt claws that are permanently extended and ridged footpads provide super traction that let this speedy cat make quick turns while chasing down its dinner.

4. *Cats always live and hunt alone. True or false? False.* While most cats prefer being alone, lions live in a family group. This group, called a pride, is usually made up of a few males plus a number of females with their young. The males defend the group and the females do the hunting. Several lionesses hunt together, tracking down and surrounding the prey. Once the females make a kill, however, the males eat first.

5. *Cats have whiskers just for looks. True or false? False.* Most cats hunt at night. So their sensitive whiskers and eyebrows help them silently feel their way. They can tell without looking, for example, if an opening is too small to squeeze through.

Make Yumdrops

Polymers, you'll remember, are long chains of molecules. You can whip up a wiggly, stretchy polymer that tastes great. Just follow these steps:

First, have an adult help you heat one-fourth cup of grape or apple juice in a saucepan on the stove until it starts to boil. Shut off the heat and sprinkle one envelope of *unflavored* gelatin over the hot liquid. Stir until the gelatin completely dissolves.

Now spread out a piece of waxed paper. Spoon nickel-sized puddles of the hot gelatin onto the paper. For an especially sweet treat, wait one minute for the gelatin to start to set up. Then sprinkle granulated sugar on each drop.

In about ten minutes, when they've completely cooled, pick up one drop. Bend it. Pull it. Twist it. See how elastic this polymer is!

Finally, pop the drop into your mouth and chew. If you can, compare your homemade yumdrop to a gumdrop you can buy at the grocery store. In what ways are the drops alike? How are they different?

Gumdrops have been a popular candy since colonial times. And they're still made much the same way today. Sugar or sweet corn syrup is mixed with gelatin or a similar substance. Then coloring and flavoring are added. Finally, this mixture is poured into molds and allowed to set. The product is the familiar elastic jelly treat.

Check out the many different flavors of gumdrops, such as orange, lemon, lime, and spearmint. In earlier times, gumdrops were also flavored with iris, ginger root, and sassafras.

To flavor your yumdrops, you could try using some of the artificial flavorings that are available at the grocery store in the baking section. What flavor do you like best?

Spider Traps

Spiders are everywhere—except Antarctica. There are about 50,000 different kinds of spiders. All of them are hunters and some are very tricky.

For example, a trap-door spider digs a burrow and spins a silk trapdoor with a hinge. Then it hides inside and waits for an insect to come close, flips open the door, and pounces.

A tropical spider called *Dinopis* spins a small web. Then it dangles from a silk line, holding the web. When an insect passes, this spider drops its net and bags its dinner.

Want to know more fascinating facts about spiders? Then this quiz is for you.

1. Spiders and insects are the same. True or false?

2. Spiders can only eat liquid food. True or false?

3. Spiders have their skeletons on the outside of their body. True or false?

4. Spiders always spin webs to catch their prey. True or false?

5. Spiders never take care of their young. True or false?

1. *Spiders and insects are the same. True or false? False.* Spiders and insects aren't even closely related. Spiders are *arachnids*, a class of animals that includes scorpions and ticks as well as spiders.

Here are some important differences to look for when deciding whether the critter is a spider or an insect: spiders have eight legs, insects only have six; spiders only have two main body parts, insects have three; spiders have leg-like structures called *palps* as sensory organs on their heads while insects have antennae.

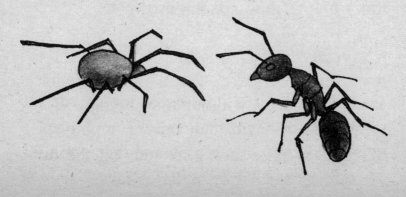

2. *Spiders can only eat liquid food. True or false? True.* Some inject their prey with digestive juices. Then they suck out the liquefied food, leaving only an empty shell of their prey. Others use their hard jaws to break up the food while pouring digestive juices over it. Then they suck up their liquid meal.

3. *Spiders have their skeletons on the outside of their body. True or false? True.* A spider's skeleton is more like a suit of armor than a supporting framework. Because it's on the outside, a spider has to shed its skeleton to grow bigger.

In this process, called molting, the skeleton splits down the back and the spider steps out. At first, its newly enlarged body is soft and weak, but the new skeleton quickly hardens. Spiders must molt seven to ten times before they are full grown.

4. *Spiders always spin webs to catch their prey. True or false? False.* Many spiders catch their prey without a web trap. Wolf spiders chase down their prey. Jumping spiders sneak up on their prey and then pounce on it. Crab spiders wait on flowers to ambush their prey. Crab spiders are even able to change color from yellow to white or white to yellow if they move to a flower of a different color.

Other ambushers look like twigs or sticks. One even looks so much like the ants on which it feeds that it can easily sneak up on its prey.

5. *Spiders never take care of their young. True or false? False.* A mother wolf spider carries her egg sac with her while the babies develop. Once they hatch, the youngsters ride on their mother's back until they're ready for a life on their own.

A mother nursery web spider sticks leaves together with silk threads to create a nursery for her hatching spiders. Then she stays nearby, guarding the nursery until the young spiders leave.

Force Water and Oil to Mix

You discovered that oil and water just naturally don't mix. When oil or an oil-base liquid is added to water, it separates, forming a layer that floats on top. This is great for printing with oil-base paints. But sometimes it's useful to have oil and water mix.

For example, if you get oily dirt on your clothes, you want to wash it off. If the oil won't mix with the water, though, it can't be washed away.

Luckily, you can wash oily dirt out of clothes with water because you can *force* oil and water to mix. You don't even have to be super strong to do it. Just try this.

First, stir two tablespoons of vegetable oil into a cup of water and wait a few minutes. Just as you expected, the oil separates and rises to float on the surface of the water.

Now add a half teaspoon of liquid dishwashing soap and stir again. Surprise! This time the oil doesn't separate. It mixes with the water.

The soap surrounds tiny droplets of oil and traps them. And since the tiny droplets can't join together to form bigger droplets that would float to the surface, they stay suspended in the water.

Soap traps all kinds of dirt particles, too. That's why it's important to rinse your hands after scrubbing with soap. How many different ways are soaps used to clean things around your home?

Make Mayonnaise

Water is not the only liquid with which oil doesn't usually mix. Oil also separates from vinegar. You may have seen oil and vinegar salad dressings that just wouldn't stay mixed. Mayonnaise, though, is a mixture in which oil and vinegar have been forced to mix by adding a third liquid.

No, the liquid that forces oil and vinegar to mix isn't liquid soap. (That's lucky since you eat mayonnaise and you wouldn't want to eat soap.) This time, the liquid that traps the oil drops in the liquid is raw egg yolk. To see this happen for yourself, follow the recipe to make some mayonnaise. Be sure to keep everything clean so you can taste the finished product.

Start by breaking two eggs into a bowl. Use a tablespoon to transfer the two yolks to another bowl. This is a little tricky, so you may want to ask an adult to help with this step. (Put the egg whites aside to use later, if you want.)

Add one-fourth teaspoon of dry mustard and one-half teaspoon of salt to the yolks. Then beat with a wire whisk until well blended.

Next, measure out one cup of vegetable oil. Pour a little of the oil — about one or two tablespoons — into the bowl. Beat this

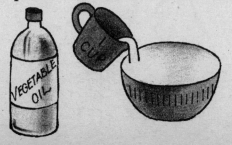

mixture with the whisk. Then pour in a little bit more oil and beat again. Keep pouring in oil, a little at a time, beating well after each addition.

After a while the mixture will get thick and creamy. When all the oil has been mixed in, add two teaspoons of vinegar and stir it in, too.

Pour the mixture into a clear glass so you can see it better. Instead of forming a separate layer floating on top, tiny droplets of

oil will remain suspended in the creamy mixture. The egg yolk coats each oil droplet, preventing it from joining other droplets to form bigger and bigger drops. Since they never form a separate layer, the tiny oil droplets are trapped.

Finally, taste the mayonnaise. How does the taste of your homemade mayonnaise compare with what you buy at the store?

Just the Bear Facts, Please

Real bears may look as soft and cuddly as toy teddy bears, but don't be fooled. Bears are tough, powerful hunters.

Pandas, by the way, aren't real bears at all. Neither are koalas. The real bears are polar bears, black bears, brown bears, spectacled bears, sun bears, and sloth bears.

Want to know some real facts about these real bears? Then take this quiz.

1. Bears only eat meat. True or false?

2. Polar bears have white fur but their skin is black. True or false?

3. Only bear cubs can climb trees. True or false?

4. The grizzly bear is California's state animal and appears on the state flag, but no wild grizzlies live in California. True or false?

5. Standing on its hind legs, Kodiak bears are taller than the tallest professional basketball player. True or false?

1. *Bears only eat meat. True or false? False.* You've probably heard the expression *hungry as a bear.* It's true. Bears eat so many different kinds of food that they are sometimes referred to as four-footed garbage disposals. These animals have sharp front teeth for cutting meat, and flat molars for grinding plants.

Bears enjoy mice, ants, fish, berries, apples, and, of course, honey. Polar bears live mainly on seals and walruses. The most important thing to a bear's diet is that there be plenty to eat.

2. *Polar bears have white fur but their skin is black. True or false? True.* Being white makes this bear camouflaged as it hunts in the snow- and ice-covered Arctic. But the special structure of its hairs and black skin keeps the polar bear warm.

Each of the bear's hairs is hollow. And these hollow hairs collect the sun's rays, directing them to the bear's skin. Because dark colors absorb sunlight better than light colors, the polar bear's black skin soaks up all available solar energy.

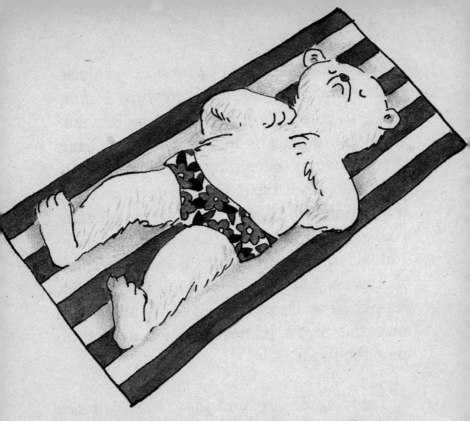

3. *Only bear cubs can climb trees. True or false? False.* Small adult bears, such as adult North American black bears, are good tree climbers. They climb trees to hunt for food and to escape danger. Big adult bears, such as grizzlies, can't climb trees, however. They are so heavy they can't pull themselves up by their claws. Since adult male grizzlies may weigh as much as 900 pounds, there are few tree limbs strong enough to support them anyway.

4. *The grizzly bear is California's state animal and appears on the state flag, but no wild grizzles live in California. True or false?* *True.* The grizzly is a kind of brown bear. There haven't been any wild grizzlies in California since the 1920s. In fact, grizzlies are considered "threatened" wherever they live. Like all types of bears, their populations have greatly decreased partly because of hunters but mainly because of builders. People have cleared large areas that were once the forest homes grizzlies needed to hunt for food.

5. *Standing on its hind legs, Kodiak bears are taller than the tallest professional basketball player. True or false?* *True.* While the tallest professional basketball players are over seven feet tall, the tallest Kodiak bears stand over nine feet tall on their hind legs.

Kodiaks are really a kind of brown bear found living on or near Kodiak Island in Alaska. These bears are also very powerful and weigh more than a half ton.

Make a Mysterious Mixture

Solids that don't dissolve in water usually sink to the bottom or rise to float on the surface.

Sometimes, though, very tiny particles of a solid that doesn't dissolve will neither sink nor float. Instead, the tiny particles remain suspended. The resulting mixture is fascinating and behaves rather mysteriously.

You can explore such a mysterious mixture firsthand. Just follow the steps for preparing one. Then perform the tests. The results are guaranteed to mystify you!

You'll need:

1¼ cups cornstarch
½ cup water
Green food coloring
   (just for fun)

Plastic garbage bag
Mixing bowl
Big metal spoon
Measuring cup

Cover your work area with the garbage bag and set the bowl on it.

Next, dump the cornstarch into the bowl.

Pour enough food coloring into the water to make it bright green.

Then add about a quarter cup of water to the cornstarch and mix well.

Add the remaining water and mix again. The mixture is just right when, as you tip the bowl, it flows but feels firm when poked with a finger.

If the mixture doesn't flow, add a little more water and stir. If it doesn't feel firm, add a little more cornstarch and stir. Keep testing and making additions of either water or cornstarch until the mysterious mixture is just right.

Now perform the following tests. Observe the results and decide if the mysterious mixture behaves more like a liquid or a solid. Then check the box on the next page to see the basic characteristics of a liquid and a solid.

1. Scoop a spoonful onto your work area. Can you break it into pieces?
2. Pick up some of the mysterious mixture. Can you shape it into a ball? Does it hold its shape?

3. Hold some in your hand and let it drip from your fingers. How do your fingers feel afterwards — wet or dry?

Don't be surprised if you find it difficult to decide if the mysterious mixture is more like a liquid or a solid. It's a little like both.

Liquids: Have a definite size but don't have a definite shape. They change shape easily.

Solids: Have a definite shape and a definite size. They don't change shape easily.

Make Fizzies

Fizzies were tablets used to produce a popular soft drink in the 1950s. When a tablet was put in water, it dissolved, creating a bubbling fruit-flavored liquid.

Like any soft drink, Fizzies got their sparkle from carbon dioxide gas that was released into the water. And just like Fizzies, you can put some nose-tickling, fizzy fun into a drink you mix up.

Most soft drinks that you buy in bottles and cans contain carbon dioxide gas that was injected into the liquid before it was sealed. As long as the drink container remains sealed and unshaken, the gas stays in solution. This means that it's mixed with the liquid so you can't tell it's there. However, as soon as the container is opened or shaken, the trapped gas starts to escape. You can see it bubbling away.

To see this for yourself, look through the side of a clear, unopened bottle of soda pop. You won't see any bubbles. But take off the cap and you'll discover lots of bubbles rushing to the surface.

To make your own Fizzies, mix these ingredients together in a cup:

1 tablespoon baking soda

2 tablespoons of Ever-Fresh, or any powder with citric acid used to keep fresh fruit from darkening after it's cut (Read the label to check the ingredients.)

6 tablespoons of powdered sugar

1 envelope (0.14 ounce) of any flavor of unsweetened powdered soft drink mix, such as Kool-Aid

Stir one heaping tablespoonful of your Fizzie powder into a juice glass full of ice water for a bubbling drink.

If you shine a flashlight through the side of the glass, you'll be able to see the bubbles of carbon dioxide gas. Or put a pinch of the powder on your tongue. You'll feel the fizz!

Carbon dioxide gas is produced any time baking soda reacts with any of a group of substances called *acids*. There are acids in many common foods. Vinegar contains acetic acid. Lemons and oranges contain citric acid. And buttermilk contains lactic acid. Adding water was all you had to do to start the chemical reaction between the baking soda and the citric acid in the Ever-Fresh.

Make a Gas-Powered Boat

You discovered that a chemical reaction between baking soda and an acid will produce carbon dioxide gas. Now you can use this science fact to power a toy boat.

To build your boat, get a plastic drink bottle with a built-in flexible straw.

Plug any openings around the straw by pressing modeling clay inside the lid.

If the straw does not have a stopper to close the end you would normally drink through, temporarily cap this with a wad of clay or chewing gum.

You are going to be producing carbon dioxide gas inside the bottle. The clay seal on the lid and the stopper on the straw will keep the gas from escaping before you're ready to let it out.

Fill a bathtub partly full of water to float your boat.

Now supply the chemical reaction that will power your boat this way:

Pour a half cup of vinegar (acetic acid) and a half cup of water into the bottle. Add a tablespoon of baking soda and quickly screw on the bottle top.

Place your bottle boat in the water. Bend the straw so the tip is just underwater and unplug the straw.

The baking soda reacts with the vinegar, producing carbon dioxide gas. The straw provides the only way for this gas to escape.

The bubbles you see are proof that the gas is escaping into the water. The carbon dioxide gas that shoots out pushes against the water. And your bottle boat moves forward in the direction that is exactly opposite this pushing force.

Be-Leaf It or Not

Would you believe that trees are the biggest living things in the world — even bigger than blue whales? They are. The tallest trees, the California redwoods, sometimes grow to heights of more than 300 feet. The heaviest trees, the giant sequoias, can weigh more than 6,000 tons. The oldest living things on earth are trees, too — bristlecone pines. In fact, there is one bristlecone pine estimated to be as much as 4,000 years old.

Are you surprised to discover these facts about trees? Then branch out and test your tree IQ.

1. The thicker the tree trunk, the older the oak tree. True or false?

2. One kind of tree is more than twice as big around as it is tall. True or false?

3. Redwoods, the tallest trees, produce the longest seed cones. True or false?

4. One really big tree can look like a whole forest. True or false?

5. You can tell a tree by its bark. True or false?

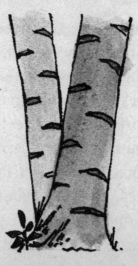

1. *The thicker the tree trunk, the older the oak tree. True or false? True.* This is actually true for most trees in temperate climates, meaning those parts of the world that have definite seasons. As the tree grows, its trunk produces two growth rings a year — a spring ring and a summer ring. The spring growth ring is lighter and usually wider. Once a tree has been cut, you can usually tell how old a tree was by counting the number of ring sets in the trunk.

It's important for trees to grow thicker trunks as they grow taller because this helps to support the spreading branches.

2. *One kind of tree is more than twice as big around as it is tall. True or false? True.* Although it is rarely more than 40 feet tall, the African baobab's trunk may be as much as 90 feet around — more than double the tree's height.

The baobab's wood is very spongy and able to absorb a lot of water. This helps the tree survive since it usually grows in very dry areas. The soft wood is easily hollowed out. People have even turned some of the bigger trees into real tree houses.

3. *Redwoods, the tallest trees, produce the longest seed cones. True or false? False.* Even though redwoods are giants, their cones are tiny — usually less than three inches long and barely an inch wide. In fact, one of these huge trees sprouts from a seed that's only about the size of a typed *o*.

4. *One really big tree can look like a whole forest. True or false? True.* One banyan tree may look like a group of trees growing close together because it has many trunk-like roots. Do you wonder why its roots aren't underground?

There's nothing usual about the way a banyan tree grows. It starts when a bird drops a banyan seed in the branches of another tree. This seed sprouts and sends roots down. The host tree eventually dies and the banyan keeps on growing bigger.

The largest banyan tree discovered so far has 350 big trunk-like roots and over 3,000 smaller ones.

5. *You can tell a tree by its bark. True or false? True.* A tree's skin is its bark. Bark helps protect the tree against insect attacks, against drying out, and sometimes even against forest fires.

Each type of tree has its own unique bark. For example, redwood bark is especially thick — as much as a foot thick — with very deep cracks. Birches, on the other hand, have paper-thin peeling bark. Pine trees have bark that flakes off in small patches as the tree grows.

It may surprise you to know that you sometimes eat bark. The spice called cinnamon that tastes so good on applesauce is made from a special kind of tree bark.

PINE   BIRCH   REDWOOD

Watch Some Raisins Dance

No, these aren't the raisin characters you may have seen dancing on television. These are raisins right out of the box or bag. And you make them dance with a chemical reaction.

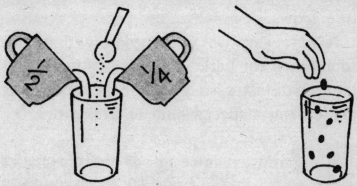

Pour a half cup of water into a tall water glass or a clear glass jar.

Stir in a quarter cup of vinegar.

Then add a teaspoon of baking soda.

As soon as the fizzing starts, signaling that the chemical reaction is in progress, drop in six raisins. The cloud of bubbles will soon

clear, and you'll be able to see your raisins rising and falling, tumbling and turning.

You have already discovered that baking soda reacting with vinegar (acetic acid) produces carbon dioxide gas. Did you guess that it is the gas bubbles that make the raisins dance?

Watch closely. You'll see gas bubbles collecting on the wrinkled raisin skins. When they have almost a solid coating of bubbles, the raisins lift off.

The raisins continue to rise until they reach the surface of the water. There, the bubbles that are exposed to the air burst, letting the carbon dioxide gas escape. And when there are no longer enough bubbles to provide support, the raisins sink.

How long do the raisins keep on dancing? Can you figure out a way to make them dance even longer?

Make an Automatic Candle Snuffer

To burn, a candle has to have oxygen. Oxygen is a gas that is commonly found in the air, and it's the gas that you must breathe in to live. Carbon dioxide gas is also commonly found in the air. It's the gas that you naturally breathe out as waste. Green plants must have carbon dioxide gas in order to make food. A candle, however, can't use carbon dioxide to burn. So if a burning candle gets more carbon dioxide than oxygen, the flame goes out.

You know how to create a chemical reaction between baking soda and an acid that will produce carbon dioxide gas. Now you'll discover how you can use this chemical reaction as a fire extinguisher to put out a candle flame without touching it.

Roll a ball of modeling clay that is about as big around as a fifty-cent piece. Gently push a birthday cake candle into the center of the ball so it stands up straight. Set the candle in its clay holder inside a juice glass or a clear plastic cup. Make sure the top of the candle wick is well below the rim of the cup.

Next, carefully spoon a tablespoon of baking soda around the base of the candle.

Set the glass in the sink for extra safety. Then have an adult light the candle. (Do *not* light it yourself!)

While the candle is burning, let a tablespoon of vinegar slide down the side of the glass into the baking soda.

As the chemical reaction takes place, you'll see the baking soda foam. The carbon dioxide gas that is produced will be invisible. But you'll be able to tell when the gas rises, engulfing the candle. The flame will go out. Poof!

Although some fire extinguishers just pump water, most use carbon dioxide in some form to put out fires. One common type, called a soda-acid extinguisher, contains bicarbonate of soda dissolved in water, and a small container of sulfuric acid. When this type of fire extinguisher is tipped upside down the chemicals mix, causing a reaction that produces carbon dioxide gas. As the pressure builds up, the gas forces the fluid out through a hose, dousing the fire.

Going Batty

Bats seem spooky because they are creatures of the night and can find their way in the dark. They even look spooky because they have sharp grasping claws, and leathery, rather than feathery, wings that spread out like a Halloween cape.

Some bats also have strange-looking faces with huge pointed ears or a wrinkled leaf-like nose. Then there is the vampire bat, which has two long, sharp front teeth, and really does live on blood.

Want to find out more about bats? Then take this quiz — FAST — before it gets dark.

1. All bats live on blood. True or false?
2. Bats are really blind. True or false?
3. One kind of bat is as big as a small rabbit. True or false?
4. Bats always live in large colonies in caves. True or false?
5. Bat babies hatch from eggs. True or false?

1. *All bats live on blood. True or false?* *False.* Only vampire bats live on blood.

Some bats eat fruit. Others eat nectar — they are important night pollinators of plants. Most bats, though, eat insects, especially mosquitoes and moths, which would otherwise be pests.

Vampire bats, by the way, are very small — less than three inches long — and only live in parts of Mexico and South America. They do not suck blood. They bite and then lap the blood that flows into the wound.

2. *Bats are really blind. True or false? False.* Bats can see. In fact, bats that eat fruit and nectar use their eyes to spot their food.

Insect-eating bats, however, don't depend on their eyesight to catch fast-darting bugs. Instead, these bats produce pulses of sounds — too high for human ears to hear — that strike objects and bounce back as echoes. Bats use these echoes to detect obstacles, tell how fast an insect is moving, and determine what direction the bug is heading.

These bats often have very large ears to pick up the echoes. Some have odd-shaped leaf-like noses that help focus the sound pulses.

3. *One kind of bat is as big as a small rabbit. True or false? True.* These bat giants are called flying foxes because they have fox-like faces. They often weigh as much as two pounds and have a wingspan stretching over five feet. Luckily, these big bats only live in hot tropical climates and only eat fruit.

The littlest bats are the Kitti's hog-nosed bats of Thailand. These bats weigh less than a penny and are as tiny as a bumblebee.

4. *Bats always live in large colonies in caves. True or false? False.* While many bats do live in caves in colonies that can number in the millions, others live alone in hollow trees, and even in barns and houses.

Wherever they roost, bats sleep hanging upside down, firmly anchored by their sharp claws.

5. *Bat babies hatch from eggs. True or false? False.* Although they can fly, bats aren't birds. They're mammals. And like other mammals, bats do not lay eggs as birds do — their young are born alive.

A baby bat is born naked but it soon grows fur. Bat babies also nurse, drinking their mother's milk, like other mammal young. Some bat babies even ride along, clinging tightly, when their mothers go hunting for food. Others are left behind clinging upside down in a sheltered spot until Mom returns.